ONE MONKEY TOO MANY

Jackie French Koller

ILLUSTRATED BY Lynn Munsinger

Harcourt Brace & Company

San Diego   New York   London

Requests for permission to make copies of any part of the work
should be mailed to: Permissions Department, Harcourt Brace & Company,
6277 Sea Harbor Drive, Orlando, Florida 32887-6777.

Library of Congress Cataloging-in-Publication Data
Koller, Jackie French.
One monkey too many/by Jackie French Koller;
illustrated by Lynn Munsinger.
p. cm.
Summary: Adventurous monkeys have a series of mishaps
and escapades involving a bike, a canoe,
a restaurant, and a hotel.
ISBN 0-15-200006-2
[1. Monkeys—Fiction.   2. Stories in rhyme.]
I. Munsinger, Lynn, ill. II. Title.
PZ8.3.K8340n 1999
[E]—dc21   96-50350

First edition
A C E F D B

Printed in Hong Kong

The illustrations in this book were done in pen and ink
and watercolor on Winsor Newton paper.
The display type was set in Fontesque Bold.
The text type was set in Goudy Catalogue.
Color separations by Bright Arts Ltd., Hong Kong
Printed by South China Printing Company, Ltd., Hong Kong
This book was printed on totally chlorine-free Nymolla Matte Art paper.
Production supervision by Stanley Redfern and Ginger Boyer
Designed by Lydia D'moch

For Ray, the Cool,
newest member of the Koller clan
—J. F. K.

For Alex, Allie, and Jack
—L. M.

"One," said the bikeman.
"This bike is for one.
One monkey can ride it,
and one can have fun."

But as soon as the bikeman
went back to his shop . . .

One monkey too many
jumped onto the bike.
One monkey too many
wheeled off down the pike.

"Hooray!" the two shouted.
"We're having such fun.
This bike is far better for two
than for one!"

Then, bingo! The bike
hit a bump in the road . . .

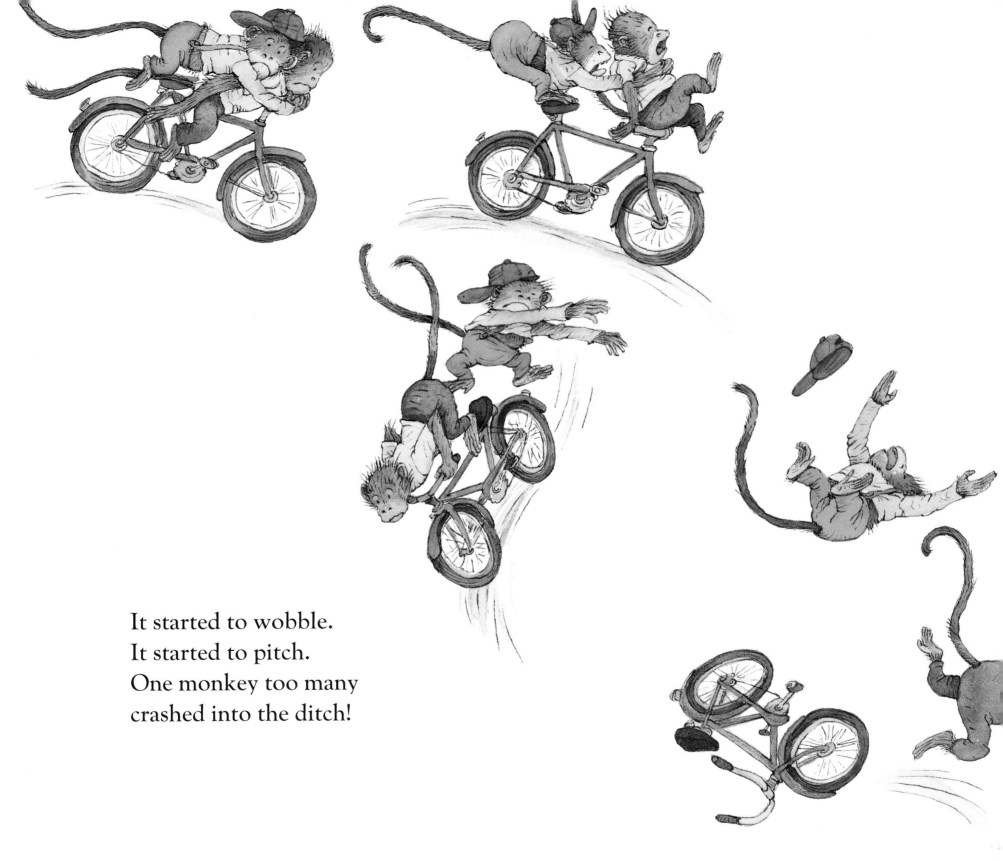

It started to wobble.
It started to pitch.
One monkey too many
crashed into the ditch!

"Two," said the golfer.
"This cart is for two.
If you're looking for fun,
this is perfect for you."

But as soon as those rascals
climbed into their seats . . .

One monkey too many
hopped up in between.
One monkey too many
rolled off 'cross the green.

"Yippee!" They all wiggled
and giggled with glee.
"This cart made for two
is fun-tastic for three!"

They zoomed up a hill
and they started back down.
Then . . .

"Oh no!" they exclaimed,
as they jammed on the brake!
One monkey too many
splashed into the lake.

"Three," said the boatman.
"This canoe is for three.
There's a seat on each end
plus one more, don't you see?"

But just as the boatman
was pushing them off . . .

One monkey too many
swung into the boat,
one monkey too many
aboard and afloat.

They paddled quite nicely
away from the shore.
"See," they said smugly,
"it's just fine with four."

But soon up ahead
came the roar of the falls . . .

"Yikes!" they all screeched,
and they tried hard to stop.
But one monkey too many
had quite a long drop.

"Four," said the waiter.
"This table's for four.
You'll be far too crowded
if you try to fit more."

But, of course, while the waiter
was getting their drinks . . .

One monkey too many
squeezed into a seat.
One monkey too many
demanded to eat.

"See here," they declared,
at the waiter's return,
"five fit just fine.
Please do not be concerned."

Then out came the dinners
and forks started flying . . .

Drinks spilled and plates tumbled,
and monkeys got rude.
One monkey too many
got covered with food.

"Five," said the bellman.
"This bed is for five.
I cannot allow
any more to arrive."

But the minute the bellman
unloaded their bags . . .

One monkey too many
poked out his small head.
One monkey too many
crept into the bed.

"See," they agreed,
with a stretch and a yawn,
"we all fit quite nicely.
The bellman was wrong."

But as soon as they started
to toss and to turn . . .

. . . to kick and to twist
and to sputter and snore,
one monkey too many
ended up in a war.

"Six," said the author.
"This book is for six.
The pages are full,
so no more of your tricks."

But that noon when the author
went out for some lunch . . .

One monkey too many came sneaking and . . .

. . . LOOK!

One monkey too many
got into this book!